"I felt like I was having a conversation with Erin that I didn't want to leave. She talked about important things in a way that I had never heard and in a way that made them real. I never felt like she was pretending to be a tween but that she understood tweens and the things we deal with and question."—Ashton, age 12

"I loved these books! They were really interesting and even answered some questions I have. I felt that the books were honest and God praising! Bravo!"—Ruth

"Erin is the kind of book I would want each of my daughters to read. It's immediately girly and attractively packaged, and Erin does a great job of drawing the reader in to her own personal faith and life story. I love that there is solid Bible teaching mixed in with fun facts from everyday life. With places for a girl to journal and reflect, the book calls for pondering and thinking deeply about living a radical life for Jesus."
—Sarah, mom of four girls

my name is

ERIN

One Girl's Plan for Radical Faith

Erin Davis

MOODY PUBLISHERS
CHICAGO

© 2013 by
ERIN DAVIS

All Scripture quotations, unless otherwise indicated, are taken from *The Holy Bible, English Standard Version.* Copyright © 2000, 2001 by Crossway Bibles, a division of Good News Publishers. Used by permission. All rights reserved.

Scripture quotations marked NIV are taken from the Holy Bible, New International Version®, NIV®. Copyright © 1973, 1978, 1984 by Biblica, Inc.™ Used by permission of Zondervan. All rights reserved worldwide. www.zondervan.com

Scripture quotations marked THE MESSAGE are from *The Message,* copyright © by Eugene H. Peterson 1993, 1994, 1995. Used by permission of NavPress Publishing Group.

All websites and phone numbers listed herein are accurate at the time of publication, but may change in the future or cease to exist. The listing of website references and resources does not imply publisher endorsement of the site's entire contents. Groups and organizations are listed for informational purposes, and listing does not imply publisher endorsement of their activities.

Edited by Annette LaPlaca
Interior and Cover design: Julia Ryan / www.DesignByJulia.com
Cover images: Shutterstock.com/Elise Gravel. Illustration of author: Julia Ryan
Interior images: Various artists/Shutterstock: frames, borders, butterfly, arrows, flowers, faces, pencil, pen, bullhorn, bee, sun, words, fish, clock, radio, earphones. Chapter illustration: Beastfromeast/iStock
Author photo: Sarah Carter Photography

Library of Congress Cataloging-in-Publication Data

Davis, Erin, 1980-
  My name is Erin : one girl's plan for radical faith : / Erin Davis.
    pages cm
  ISBN 978-0-8024-0645-3
1. Preteens--Religious life--Juvenile literature. 2. Teenage girls--Religious life--Juvenile literature. 3. Christian life--Juvenile literature.
I. Title.
  BV4551.3.D36 2013
  248.8'33--dc23
                            2013013190

We hope you enjoy this book from Moody Publishers. Our goal is to provide high-quality, thought-provoking books and products that connect truth to your real needs and challenges. For more information on other books and products written and produced from a biblical perspective, go to www.moodypublishers.com or write to:

Moody Publishers
820 N. LaSalle Boulevard
Chicago, IL 60610

1 3 5 7 9 10 8 6 4 2

Printed in the United States of America

To the baby who grew in me as I wrote this book.
May you live a radical life for Jesus.

Contents

CHAPTER 1

Radical

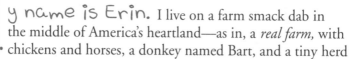**y name is Erin.** I live on a farm smack dab in the middle of America's heartland—as in, a *real farm,* with chickens and horses, a donkey named Bart, and a tiny herd of goats. In many ways my life is pretty average. I love my family. I love my job. I love my church. I have the best friends a girl could ask for and when they're not available, a chick flick and a bowl of popcorn (extra butter, please) are welcome to keep me company any time. At first glance, my life seems just like everyone else's. But look closer, and I hope you'll see that there's something different about me (and I'm not just talking about all the livestock!).

I wish I could invite every reader of this book over for a visit. We'd take  a hayride and roast marshmallows over a bonfire, and I'd tell you about my journey from being a girl who knew about God to being a girl who knew God to being a girl who let God turn her life upside down.

Erin's List of the Top Five Chick Flicks of All Time

- The Princess Bride
- Gone with the Wind
- My Girl
- Steel Magnolias
- The Little Mermaid

9

I'd tell you I'm not interested in just having faith in Jesus. I don't just want to check the box for Christian, like crossing chores off a to-do list, and then blend in with the crowd. I want a radical faith that changes everything about my life. I want you to have a radical faith too.

rad*i*cal:
very different from the usual or traditional.[1]

What do you think of when you hear the word *radical*? Do you imagine someone who dresses weird, talks weirder, and seems to do whatever it takes to stick out like a sore thumb? Is a radical someone who carries picket signs or marches for a cause she's passionate about? What about standing up for your faith, even if it costs you? Is that what it takes to be radical?

All of those things are unconventional, but you don't necessarily have to dress strange or stage a sit-in to be radical. In fact, the Bible is chock-full of radical followers of God. We'll look at many of their stories in the pages of this book, but you don't have to time travel into the Old Testament Promised Land or New Testament Palestine to find people with radical faith. If radical simply means different from the usual, then any of us who are willing to be shaped into the image of Jesus can fit the bill.

I won't sugarcoat it—radical faith has its challenges. But Jesus went first. He showed us what a radical life, lived for God's glory, looks like. Then He simply says, "Follow Me," down the path He's already taken.

I've been a non-Christian, a lukewarm Christian, and a Christian on fire to live like God calls me to. Which is the best way to live? The answer is a no-brainer. Once you've experienced radical life in Christ, nothing else will satisfy.

My name is Erin, and this is my story.

This Changes Everything

I grew up going to church. I knew all about baby Jesus in the manger and baby Moses in the basket. I could sing "Father Abraham" and "Deep and Wide" with the best of them, but I never thought much about how that fountain flowing deep and wide could impact my life or why I was one of Father Abraham's "many sons."

"Deep and Wide" may be describing the fountain of Christ's love described in this passage: "And I pray that you, being rooted and established in love, may have power, together with all the Lord's holy people, to grasp how wide and long and high and deep is the love of Christ" (Ephesians 3:17–18 NIV). Find out why you are a daughter of Abraham in Genesis 22.

Jesus was someone I talked about at church, but that's usually where I left Him. I believed He existed, but I didn't put my hope in Him or allow His Word to influence the way I lived my life.

That all changed the summer before my sophomore year of high school.

My family decided to check out a new church on a Sunday morning. We had been barely attending a sluggish church in my small town before then. I never heard much that seemed to apply to my life, and frankly, everyone looked kind of miserable. I often wondered if trusting Jesus meant turning in my smile in exchange for a frown. But as the worship music keyed up at the new church, something seemed . . . different. The pastor preached with passion from the Word of God, and what he said felt important.

After the service the youth pastor came up and invited me to join the youth group on a trip to camp leaving the next morning. Looking back, I'm surprised I said yes. It meant hopping on a bus with people I'd never met to learn more about a God I had kept at arm's length, but the next day I loaded my suitcase onto the bus along with seventeen other teenagers and began a twelve-hour bus ride toward a radical change.

The very first night of camp, I felt overwhelmed by the love of God and the reality of my own sinfulness. It was suddenly clear that serving Him wasn't about being a good girl or being in church every time the doors were open. God wasn't interested in giving me a to-do list. Clearly, if I wanted to follow Christ, I needed a radical change of heart. It was as if God wanted to perform open-heart surgery on me in that camp sanctuary, taking out the parts of me that wanted to just skate through life and replacing them with a vibrant love and passion for Him.

Maybe you've had a moment like that—a time in your history when God did something radical in your own heart. Putting your faith and trust in Him certainly feels like taking a giant leap, but really it's just the beginning of the exciting, and—yes—radical journey that comes with agreeing to live as God calls you to.

Take a moment to write about a time when God called you to radical change.

_____

_____

_____

_____

🌸 Roll Call of Radicals

Meet Elijah. Elijah was a prophet assigned to warn his people about God's anger because of their worship over the false god Baal. Elijah gave his prediction of a drought to the wicked leader of his day and then fled to live by a brook for several months. There he was fed by ravens—as in, birds literally delivered his breakfast, lunch, and dinner. When the brook dried up, Elijah obeyed God's voice again and went to live with a widow he did not know. When her son got sick, Elijah lay on him three times and the boy was healed (1 Kings 17). Later Elijah confronted the prophets of Baal and called down fire from heaven (1 Kings 18). At the end of his ministry, Elijah was taken up into heaven in a whirlwind of fiery chariots and horses (2 Kings 2:11).

Nothing Elijah did fit the mold of a normal life. Today we might call him "eccentric" or say that Elijah was an outcast. But Elijah wasn't just different for *different's* sake. Elijah listened closely to the voice of God. When God told Elijah to move to a brook, he did. When God told him to ask a stranger for food and shelter, he did. When God asked Elijah to confront the prophets of Baal, Elijah did it, even though he was outnumbered 450 to 1. When God sent chariots of fire and horses to Elijah at the end of his life, Elijah got caught up in the whirlwind.

Elijah was a radical.

Joshua was born as a slave in Egypt. He became a conqueror in the Promised Land. When Moses sent twelve spies to scope out the land God promised them, most of them came back shaking in their boots because they saw big challenges. Joshua, however, was ready to charge in full speed. He knew God had his back (Numbers 13). But because Joshua was in the minority, his people were forced to wander for forty years. Of the twelve spies, only Joshua and Caleb (who also thought they should take the Promised Land) survived long enough to live in the land of milk and honey (Numbers 14).

Joshua went on to become Moses's successor. He led his people in several military campaigns, including the strange battle of Jericho, where their military strategy was to walk in circles and blow trumpets. Because Joshua obeyed, they won the battle without ever lifting a sword (Joshua 6)!

Joshua goes down in history as a radical because of his unwavering trust in God. He obeyed God even when it was unpopular or untraditional. Following God when no one else does—now that's radical!

How about Paul? Paul strikes me as a man of extremes. When we first meet him in the book of Acts his name is Saul and he is supervising the death of Stephen (another radical!). In fact, Saul led a campaign to kill and imprison Christians. Acts 8:3 tells us that "Saul was ravaging the church, and entering house after house, he dragged off men and women and committed them to prison."

I guess radical isn't always a good thing.

But then Saul had a truly radical encounter with God. Acts 9 tells the story of Saul's conversion from radical against Jesus to a radical for Jesus. He was walking on the road to Damascus, on his way to find more Christians to throw into jail, when God struck him blind. Sometimes God has to take radical measures to get our attention! God Himself spoke to Saul and asked him why he was persecuting Him (because when you mess with Jesus' followers, you mess with Him).

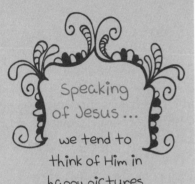

In the face of such a dramatic encounter, Paul chose to acknowledge that Jesus was Lord. Then his life got really radical. He made three long missionary journeys, planting churches and sharing the radical message of the gospel. I told you that radical life will likely cost you. It certainly cost Paul. He endured prison, beatings, shipwrecks, threats, and hunger in order to follow God. But a radical counts the cost and serves God anyway.

In Philippians 3:7–8 Paul wrote, "But whatever gain I had, I counted as loss for the sake of Christ. Indeed, I count everything as loss because of the surpassing worth of knowing Christ Jesus my Lord. For his sake I have suffered the loss of all things and count them as rubbish, in order that I may gain Christ."

Paul said nothing compares to being a radical for Christ. In fact, everything else is rubbish, garbage, destined for the trash heap. Paul reached radical status because of his encounter with the most radical one of all—Jesus.

16

Speaking of Jesus . . . we tend to think of Him in happy pictures with a perpetual smile on his face. We imagine Him as a baby in a manger or in flowing robes with children on His lap. Those images are part of Jesus' life, but the bigger picture is much more, well, radical!

Maybe you've heard of the Pharisees and the Sadducees? We hear about them often in the New Testament. They were the religious leaders while Jesus was alive. If following God were about following rules, these guys would be spiritual superstars, but their hearts were rotten. Jesus was always blasting them for trying to follow God by checking off a long to-do list of rules while ignoring their own sin. These guys were the current "big dogs" of the faith, and Jesus faced them down. That was certainly radical.

Then there's Jesus' team. He assembled a ragtag bunch of average Joes to help Him spread the radical message that He was God's Son. These guys were not pastors. They didn't have degrees from Bible college. But they were willing to be radical for the cause of Christ. That was the only thing Jesus looked at when He examined their resumes.

Once He had a team of radicals assembled, Jesus really shook things up. He started healing and preaching and hanging out with tax collectors and prostitutes. People were so shocked by how different Jesus was that they usually had one of two reactions. Either they abandoned everything to follow Him, or they determined to do whatever it took to stop Him.

Jesus said all kinds of radical things, like "If anyone comes to me and does not hate his own father and mother and wife and children and brothers and sisters, yes, and even his own life, he cannot be my disciple"

(Luke 14:26), and "Do not think that I have come to bring peace to the earth. I have not come to bring peace, but a sword" (Matthew 10:34). He even said, "If anyone would come after me, let him deny himself and take up his cross daily and follow me" (Luke 9:23).

Jesus wasn't inviting everyone to sit around a bonfire and sing a happy song. Sure He preached about God's love, but He didn't come to earth to give everyone a giant, warm, fuzzy feeling. His message was radical. We are sinners. Our sin keeps us from God. And He, the one and only Son of God, had come to pay the price for that sin. But following Him will cost us.

Now that's radical.

 Spotting a Radical

What do these radicals from the pages of the Bible have in common?

 They trusted God.

 They listened to God's voice and then obeyed—even when it cost them.

 Because of their faith, they lived lives that looked different from everyone else's.

That's a short list and a tall order, but basically it means you can be a radical too. There's nothing on that list that is impossible for you. There's nothing on that list that requires you to be older, more financially stable, or have a college degree. No matter who you are or where you live you can live a radical faith.

The rest of this book is highly practical. You'll have the chance to discover what a radical faith might look like for you. But you have to take the first step and trust God that the life He calls you to is the very best way to live.

With that in mind, take some time to ask God to show you His radical plan for your life. It might sound something like this:

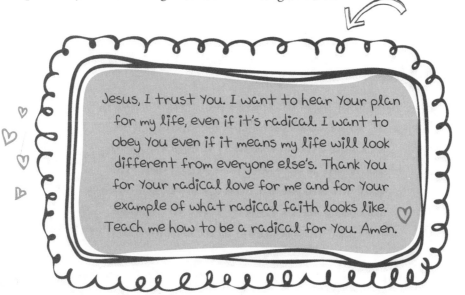

Jesus, I trust You. I want to hear Your plan for my life, even if it's radical. I want to obey You even if it means my life will look different from everyone else's. Thank You for Your radical love for me and for Your example of what radical faith looks like. Teach me how to be a radical for You. Amen.

CHAPTER 2

But I Still
Have Math
Homework

 id you know this book is actually the fourth book in a series of books about living out the Truth found in God's Word? If you haven't read the other three books, you can check them out at erindavis.org. In the meantime, I'll give you a crash course.

My Name Is Erin: One Girl's Journey to Discover Truth is a book about the Bible. Here are three big takeaways:

1. God's Word works like a belt. It protects us. It guards us. It helps us fight big battles.

2. God's Word is like a filter. We can squeeze the tough questions of life through it and come up with answers every time.

3. God's Word is like a tether. It keeps us connected to God Himself.

My Name Is Erin: One Girl's Journey to Discover Who She Is explains some of the unique ways God designed men and women. It's chock-full of good stuff about what it means to be a godly girl, but the big lesson is this—the reason girls are girls and guys are guys is to reveal something about God.

Be sure to check out the other books at erindavis. org.

My Name Is Erin: One Girl's Mission to Make a Difference tells about my personal journey to live out the mission God has for me. For me, that means teaching God's Word to young women like you. For you, that might mean raising money for a missions organization, getting involved in a cause to help abused and neglected children, or building relationships with the truly lonely in your community. The bottom line is that God has a mission for you (should you choose to accept it).

These are big ideas!

If the Bible is a filter you should squeeze your entire life through, that's a game changer. If God designed you to make Him famous, that should impact the way you look at yourself. If God has a big mission for you, that makes the little stuff of life seem, well, a little less important.

If you decide to let the Bible change how you live, the transformation will be—you guessed it—radical!

Lukewarm Living

Can you be a Christian and not be a radical? I suppose it's possible, but why would you want to? That kind of living reminds me of God's words to the church in Laodicea recorded in the book of Revelation: "I know your works: you are neither cold nor hot. Would that you were either cold or hot! So, because you are lukewarm, and neither hot nor cold, I will spit you out of my mouth" (Revelation 3:15–16).

Imagine a mouthful of room-temperature water for a moment. Blech. Now think of ice-cold water on a hot day. Yum! What about a steaming cup of hot tea on a snowy afternoon? Now you're talking! But lukewarm water? There's nothing thrilling about that.

But that's how God describes the people in the Laodicean church: like lukewarm water. Sure, they went to church. They even did some good stuff for God, but they had no passion. They didn't stand out. They loved business as usual. Clearly, God does not.

The Gab Gallery!

The church in Laodicea reminds me of a group of girls we interviewed for this book. These were great girls, growing up in big cities and small towns. They loved to talk, which is why I have affectionately nicknamed them the Gab Gallery. From here on out I will just call them "the Gallery."

The girls we met are Christian girls. Many of them are involved in their church youth groups. They wear Christian T-shirts; they listen to Christian music. But to be honest, most of the time their lives look just like everyone else's.

The Gallery girls had a sideline mentality about doing big things with their faith. They read their Bibles and went to church, but that didn't result in radical change.

I spend a lot of time with young Christian women, and I've found that most of them are like the Gallery in this way. I see young women who read the Bible but don't tie their lives to it. I see girls who have no idea why God created men and women, and so they struggle with relationships, and family, and their role in it all. I see Christians of all ages who have no idea that God wants to use them to accomplish a big mission. I wrestle with my own tendency to want to just coast, to live like a cup of room-temperature water instead of being on fire for God. Sigh.

What's keeping us from the radical faith God calls us to?

Roadblocks to Radical

I was recently on a tour with a team of other speakers. We traveled from city to city speaking to moms and daughters about the radical choice to live pure lives. Every single night the altar was filled with crying teenage girls. Many of them knelt in front of the altar and sobbed, completely brokenhearted. Why?

Some of the Gallery girls were facing sin they wanted to deal with. Others were wrestling with pain from their pasts. But night after night after night I counseled girls who were broken by two unlikely roadblocks to radical faith: busyness and prayerlessness.

These girls cried big fat tears because schoolwork and sports and after-school clubs were deafening them to the voice of God. They didn't have time to pray. They certainly didn't have time to listen. They had volleyball practice, for goodness sake!

I can see one girl as clear as day in my mind. She must have been about thirteen. Her head was so buried in her hands at the altar that I could not see her eyes. When I asked her, "How can I pray for you?" it seemed to take her forever to look up. Through sobs she finally choked out, "I . . . can't . . . get . . . my . . . math . . . homework . . . done."

I'm not trying to belittle her problem or say that math homework doesn't matter, but I was shocked that homework was the issue that had tied her heart up in knots. I asked what would happen if she didn't get her math homework done. She said she would fail the assignment. I asked what would happen if she failed the assignment. She said her grade would drop. I asked what her grade would be then, and she said, "Maybe a B." Then she started sobbing again.

Other girls confided that they were so wrapped up in schoolwork, church work, family responsibilities, hanging out with friends, sports, and clubs that they had zero time to nurture their relationship with God. Sure, they had full schedules, but their hearts were empty. Their faith was barely limping along.

When we asked the Gallery how they were preparing for the future, their answers sounded a lot like a college entrance essay. They mentioned studying, sports, developing people skills, learning to be a leader—but none of them mentioned deepening their relationship with God, studying His Word, or seeking His plan for the future. Clearly, a life based on achievements and goals is the norm, but a life based on God is increasingly radical.

I wonder if busyness and prayerlessness are roadblocks to a radical faith in your life. Are you so wrapped up in getting the usual stuff done that you don't have time for the radical stuff only God can assign?

✿ The Pressure Cooker

In many ways life for the average middle school and high school girl has started to resemble a pressure cooker. Here's why.

★ Because of the pressure to get into a good college, you may have opted to take advanced placement (AP) classes. Experts say each AP class will likely result in forty-five minutes of homework every single school night. If you're in three AP classes—say, AP English, AP Biology, and AP Math—you can expect to spend almost two and a half hours doing homework after an eight-hour school day.

26

★ Twenty-three percent of you spend two to five hours per day practicing a sport or musical instrument.

★ Twenty-one percent of you spend at least ten hours a week working for pay.

★ Most of you are spending between two and ten hours per week hanging out with your friends.[3]

I'm sure you're tired from all of that homework; so let me do the math for you. Each week you have 168 hours to spend. Between school, sports, and friends you've spent as many as eighty hours of that time. Add in some time for sleep, and you've ticked away 133 of your hours. Now factor in time with your family, involvement at church, and time for good, old-fashioned fun, and the numbers can stop adding up. You've only got twenty-four hours in every day, and yet you may be juggling more than your day can hold.

That's why coming across verses like this one may really make you feel the pressure: "Be still, and know that I am God. I will be exalted among the nations, I will be exalted in the earth!" (Psalm 46:10).

How can you be still when there is so much going on? How can you know God when your schedule feels ready to burst at the seams? How can you have a radical faith when so much of your day is spent just trying to survive business as usual?

Warning: Radical amputation may be necessary.

27

🌸 First Things First

In Matthew 6 we find Jesus preaching His famous Sermon on the Mount. Crowds of people had been following Him. Jesus seized the opportunity to teach a captive audience, and He sat down on a mountain and talked about the things of God.

Jesus covered all kinds of important topics in this sermon, but we are going to zero in on two key themes.

Jesus said, "Do not lay up for yourselves treasures on earth, where moth and rust destroy and where thieves break in and steal, but lay up for yourselves treasures in heaven, where neither moth nor rust destroys and where thieves do not break in and steal. For where your treasure is, there your heart will be also" (Matthew 6:19–21).

> Check out the complete Sermon on the Mount in Matthew 5-7.

Jesus was teaching two important lessons. First, our treasures have a way of consuming our hearts. They occupy our affections. We love what we treasure most. The opposite is also true. If we want to know what our treasure is, we just need to look at our own hearts. Whatever we love the most is our treasure.

Jesus also taught us not to treasure things that won't last. This could be stuff like iPads, clothes, cars, and jewelry. But it could be other things that cannot last, like popularity, awards, or accomplishments.

I struggle to treasure the right things. I tend to love compliments, achievement, and pretty things more than I love living like God calls me to. When I treasure the wrong things, my heart gets off track. Jesus knew I would struggle with this, which is why He kindly warned me that the things I'm tempted to love cannot last.

Where is your treasure? What is it that you value? You can find the answer by looking at your heart. Here are some questions to get you started.

★ What do you spend most of your time thinking about?

★ What do you spend most of your money on?

★ If you lost _____, you would feel like you couldn't go on.

★ What/Who do you love most in the world?

★ What does the way you spend your time reveal about what you treasure most?

Jesus knew that our hearts would get wrapped up in the wrong kinds of treasure. That's why He went on to warn us to keep first things first.

Jesus said, "Therefore do not be anxious, saying, 'What shall we eat?' or 'What shall we drink?' or 'What shall we wear?' For the Gentiles seek after all these things, and your heavenly Father knows that you need them all. But seek first the kingdom of God and his righteousness, and all these things will be added to you" (Matthew 6:31–33).

Jesus is telling us to stop sweating the small stuff. If you were sitting on that mountain with Him, He might say, "Stop freaking out about that grade, or that friend, or whether or not your basketball team will win districts."

Then He offers a simple alternative to the chaos: "Seek first the kingdom of God."

Make God your first priority. Listen to His voice before you listen to anyone else's. Start your day with Him. Plan your schedule around Him. Treasure His will above anything else. That is the simple formula for radical faith.

The psalmist put it this way: "Whom have I in heaven but you? And there is nothing on earth that I desire besides you" (Psalm 73:25).

I like how *The Message* paraphrases this verse: "You're all I want in heaven! You're all I want on earth!"

The radical choice that nothing matters more than God is what motivated Elijah to take on the prophets of Baal. He was willing to risk his reputation and his popularity because those did not matter more than God. Seeking God's kingdom first is what made Joshua a radical. Most of the other spies got caught up in worry. They saw big giants in the Promised Land, and they were anxious. But Joshua sought God's kingdom first. He knew that if God was on their side, no giant was too big for them. He was willing to charge into battle with giants because God's kingdom was his first priority. After encountering God, Paul decided nothing mattered more than Him. He gave up comfort. He gave up power. He gave up acceptance because he treasured God's kingdom above all else.

There are many, many other radicals in the Bible and in the pages of history. Esther risked death to save her people, because standing up for God's kingdom meant more than living a safe life. John the Baptist lived in the wilderness and let others make fun of him because God's kingdom was more important than fitting in. Mother Teresa spent her entire life caring for the sick and needy because God's Word asked her to. Jim Elliot was a missionary who risked everything to share Jesus with a violent tribe in Ecuador. Warriors from that tribe killed Jim and four other missionaries. Jim knew the risks, and yet he paid the ultimate price to share Christ because God was his treasure.

These radicals show us a painful truth: If you want radical faith, you will have to amputate those things that compete with God to be your greatest treasure.

Remember how I told you that busyness and prayerlessness were two huge roadblocks to radical faith among the girls I know? That shouldn't have surprised me. Those two things kept me locked out from radical living for years.

Sure, I decided to follow God at camp when I was fifteen, but it was a long time before I made the time to live a life that looked different from my life before Christ. I was too busy being busy.

I was too busy being busy.

I still fight being boxed in by busyness and the nasty side effects of prayerlessness and failing to read the Bible. I've had to get pretty radical to elevate my relationship with Jesus above everything else that tends to pull on me. I don't own a television. I don't have a Facebook account. I say no to activities and events a lot more often than I say yes. That isn't because I want to create a bunch of rules for myself or because I believe God has rules for me. I think it's possible to be a radical Christian and own a TV or be on Facebook. But for *me* to have room in my heart and my life to let God really change me, I had to get serious about amputating those things that kept me stuck in business as usual.

While radical amputation can be painful, the results are always worth it. Don't believe me? Allow me to shift your focus toward some radicals you admire.

Use the prompts below to make profiles of individuals whose faith you admire. They can be people you know personally, people you've encountered or heard about, or people in the Bible.

Name: _____

How can you tell this person's faith matters?

_____

_____

🦋 What makes this person radical (i.e., different from everyone else)?

_____

_____

_____

🦋 Do you see any benefits of radical faith in this person's life?

_____

_____

_____

The people living radical lives for Christ are often the people we admire most. They challenge us. They inspire us. They make us want to be more like Jesus.

Wouldn't you love for others to say that *you* make them want to be more like Christ? Wouldn't it be amazing if God used you to do big things for His kingdom? Doesn't a life lived differently from the usual seem exciting, even if there are risks?

❀ Making Room

You can have a radical faith because God does all the heavy lifting. You don't have to drum up a mission or beg God to use you. He wants to make you more like Him. He wants to use you to reach a lost and dying world. But you do have to decide that He is the most important thing. It's a radical step, for sure.

I don't know how God wants to change you, but I do know that radical faith starts with the not so radical step of making time to learn from God. If you are going to hear from Him and respond, you need wiggle room in your life. You can't cram every spare moment with responsibilities and activities and expect to find space to grow a radical faith.

Think back to those radicals you admire. I'm sure they are busy doing good things, but I bet if you ask them they also make prayer a priority. I'm sure they'd tell you that reading their Bible is one of the most important things they do every day—and often the first thing they do each morning. That's because they've created margins for God to work.

That's where I'd like you to start. Take a hard look at your life, specifically your schedule, and look for ways you can create space for God to move. Here's a tool to help you.

Use these code letters (or come up with your own) to fill in times where you can squeeze in a little more time with the Lord.

♡ P=Pray   ♡ RB=Read my Bible
♡ J=Journal ♡ W=Worship through song

♡	Monday	Tuesday	Wednesday	Thursday	Friday	Saturday	Sunday
8 a.m.							
9 a.m.							
10 a.m.							
11 a.m.							
12 p.m.							
1 p.m.							
2 p.m.							
3 p.m.							
4 p.m.							
5 p.m.							
6 p.m.							
7 p.m.							
8 p.m.							
9 p.m.							
10 p.m.							

✿ Choosing the Right Rocks

I realize there are things that just have to be done. Don't you dare tell your parents I said you didn't have to do your math homework because you are learning to have radical faith! But my guess is there are some time stealers that keep you stuck in business as usual instead of preparing to do something bigger. There may also be some good stuff on your schedule that isn't good enough to compete with making God "all you want on earth."

I once heard a youth pastor talk about making God a priority using a jar and a bunch of rocks. First he just tried to cram all the rocks into the jar willy-nilly. They didn't all fit. So he dumped them out. Then he purposefully put the biggest rocks in the jar first, followed by the medium-sized rocks, and topped with the tiny pebbles. The tiny pebbles slid down into the spaces left between the larger rocks. Amazingly, every last rock crammed into the jar.

Remember the Sermon on the Mount, where Jesus reminded us that our treasure is tied to our hearts? During that same sermon, He said this: "But seek first the kingdom of God and his righteousness, and all these things will be added to you" (Matthew 6:33).

The "things" Jesus promised would be added were clothes and food, but you can substitute anything you think you can't live without. Maybe for you it's popularity, achievement, security, or technology. What does Jesus say you should do when those things dampen the fire of your faith down to lukewarm status?

$\longrightarrow$ "Seek first the kingdom."

In other words, make God your number-one priority. And the other stuff—the little stuff, those tiny pebbles that fill up your life—will fall into place.

For me, radical faith began with making changes to the ordinary. It started when I decided to plan my time around seeking God instead of seeking God in the nooks and crannies of my days.

Do you want a faith that others admire? Do you want a life that makes a difference? You can take a giant leap in that direction today simply by putting first things first.

What are some "small pebbles" you can cut out of your life, to make more room for God? Write about those things in a letter to God below.

Dear God, _____

_____

_____

_____

_____

_____

_____

CHAPTER 3

Ditching
Dead Fish

G rab a bottle of sunscreen and a towel! We're about to take a trip to the lake.

In Matthew 4 we find Jesus, who has just returned from forty days in the wilderness where He faced near-relentless attacks from Satan yet He did not sin. Instead, He prayed and sought God's direction for the mission God had for Him.

You might say Jesus was putting first things first. His life was about to ramp up to warp speed. Soon there would be people to minister to, sermons to preach, sick people to heal. But before all that . . . Jesus spent time with the Father.

Jesus put the biggest rocks in the jar before dealing with the "little" stuff. He sought first the kingdom. And then . . . He headed into town to begin His radical ministry.

We pick the story up there, on the shore of a lake.

> While walking by the Sea of Galilee, he saw two brothers, Simon (who is called Peter) and Andrew his brother, casting a net into the sea, for they were fishermen.

Jesus put the biggest rocks in the jar before dealing with the "little" stuff. He sought first the kingdom. And then . . . He headed into town to begin His radical ministry. ♡

And he said to them, "Follow me, and I will make you fishers of men." Immediately they left their nets and followed him. And going on from there he saw two other brothers, James the son of Zebedee and John his brother, in the boat with Zebedee their father, mending their nets, and he called them. Immediately they left the boat and their father and followed him. (Matthew 4:18–22)

If we fast-forward a bit, we see that this was just the beginning of a radical adventure for Peter, Andrew, James, and John. They became the first four of the twelve disciples who served as Jesus' right-hand men as He changed the world forever.

Peter, James, and John witnessed the transfiguration. If you're not familiar with that story, check it out in Matthew 17. Jesus took His friends up onto a mountain where He was transfigured (that's a fancy word for *changed*) into a glowing man with a face that "shone like the sun" and clothes that "became white as light." Then He had a chat with Moses and Elijah, even though they had both been dead for hundreds of years! How cool is that? It's like something out of a sci-fi movie, and Peter, James, and John had front row seats!

These disciples were also among the first to hear about Jesus' plans. They had insider knowledge about His radical rescue mission. Jesus picked Peter to be the "rock" to build His church on (Matthew 16:18). God used Peter to accomplish a huge mission.

The disciples lived lives that mattered. They had an all-access pass to the Savior of the whole world! They saw Him work miracles. They ate with Him. They were chosen by Him to change history forever. But it all started with the radical choice to abandon everything else.

✿ Radical Faith versus Dead Fish

Let's backtrack a bit. Jesus sees Peter and Andrew fishing. When Jesus found them, they were having just another day at work. Then He gives them a simple command: "Follow me."

We know the end of the story. We have the cheat sheet that shows us Jesus really was God and He was going to use Peter and Andrew for big stuff, but they didn't have access to that information. They simply saw a man on the shore asking them to follow Him—and they dropped everything and did it. Now that's radical!

The Bible says they left their nets, but they left much more than that. They left their jobs, their ticket to security. I'm pretty sure they also left their reputations there on the beach. I doubt many people understood how they could leave their nets and follow Jesus without a ten-year plan. They may have lost family members and friends who shook their heads in disgust at what seemed like an irresponsible decision.

What about James and John? The Bible says, "Immediately they left the boat and their father and followed him" (Matthew 4:22). In other words, they walked away from everything. I wonder what their father said as they ditched the family fishing business to follow a stranger on the beach. Did he worry? Did he yell? Did stomp his feet and say, "You come back here this minute"? The Bible doesn't say, but we can be sure the choice to follow Jesus cost James and John plenty.

Being a radical for Jesus will cost you too. I know I've said that often in this book, but I don't want you to miss that point. There's a reason why lukewarm Christianity is so tempting—it requires so little from us. To keep water cold or hot, you have to work at it. You either need to keep adding ice or keep adding heat. For lukewarm water, you can just let your cup sit on the counter. It requires no effort, no time, no energy. Effortless faith may sound appealing, but think about what's really at stake.

What if Peter, Andrew, James, and John had told Jesus no that day? Yep, life might have gone a little smoother. Sure, people might have snickered a little less. But on their best day all they would have to show for their lives would be a boatload of dead fish. That's it. No lives changed. No earth-shaking mission. No intimacy with Jesus. Just day after day of dead fish.

The Big Flip

Imagine you're on the fishing boat with the first disciples. You're minding your own business, tending to all of those fish, when a figure appears on the beach. You squint to get a better look at Him, but He doesn't seem familiar. Suddenly, you lock eyes.

"Uh, hi," you say.

"Follow Me," He answers.

Follow Me? What does that mean? It's a message that is especially hard for us to understand because we usually get it backward. If you're anything like me, you might be tempted to look at Jesus on the horizon and say, "Follow *me*."

We tend to want Jesus to tag along as we live life our own way. We don't mind if He shows up with us at church every once in a while or meets with us when we have time for Him. But we want to take the lead.

Follow me onto the boat, Jesus.
Follow me into my life.
Follow me into the future I have planned.
Follow me as I live a lukewarm faith.

But we've got it all wrong. Faith in Christ isn't about throwing on a Christian T-shirt as we go on doing our own thing. It's not about running our own lives and inviting Jesus to come along. It requires a major flip. Before we decide to follow Christ, we may be in the lead. But when we've truly encountered Him, we must turn on our heels and follow Him. He gets to run the show. We get to become followers.

It's a truth I didn't understand for a long time. I became a Christian at age fifteen, but then I just kept marching down the path I'd always been on. I asked Jesus to "follow me" as I continued to make my own plans for the future and live like I wanted to. The only

43

To keep water cold or hot, you have to work at it. You either need to keep adding ice or keep adding heat. For lukewarm water, you can just let your cup sit on the counter. It requires no effort, no time, no energy.

difference was that I went to church more and listened to secular music a little less. But I hadn't left my boat yet. I was still shuffling stinky fish.

It wasn't until well after college, when I had been a Christian for more than a decade, that I understood following God meant my life needed to look different (i.e., radical) because I followed Jesus.

In fact, the Bible says we should look like aliens visiting a strange planet: "Dear friends, I urge you, as aliens and strangers in the world, to abstain from sinful desires, which war against your soul" (1 Peter 2:11 NIV).

That passage isn't talking about looking like little green extraterrestrials. It's giving us the image of being a stranger, a foreigner, someone who looks and acts different from the people around her because this is not home.

There have been times when I felt God asking me to make decisions that made no sense from a logical perspective. In those situations, my choice is to follow God or try to run my own show. In the same way, it's a constant battle for me to guard my heart. My default is to look at Hollywood and think that, because my life looks cleaner than the superstars in our culture, I am free to dabble in what the world has to offer. But then I remember that God's Word is my filter. When I squeeze my choices through it, I find verses like this one: "Be holy, because I am holy" (1 Peter 1:16 NIV). Then I realize that Jesus should be my standard. There have been times when God has asked me to give up something important to me. I've had to choose whether or not I will abandon ship or keep my grip on dead fish.

Over and over, I have to choose whether I will listen to Jesus' invitation to follow Him or keep doing my own thing and hope He tags along.

 Are You a Radical?

Did you know Peter, Andrew, James, and John went back to their boats? We find them fishing often in the New Testament. That means they had to choose radical faith over and over again.

Normal life has a way of tugging at us. It pulls us back to the familiar and away from letting Jesus lead. That's why radical faith isn't a choice you make once. Every day you will face the choice to hold tightly to your old life or listen to Jesus when He says, "Follow Me."

How can you know if you're still on the boat?

Take a look around you. Is there anything about your life that looks different from the lives of the non-Christians you know? Write about that below.

_____

_____

_____

_____

_____

Do a little time travel in your mind. Think back to before you were a Christian. How has your life changed since then? Has the change been dramatic, or is there evidence that you've been sticking to business as usual?

Before I was a Christian I . . .

_____

_____

_____

After I became a Christian I . . .

_____

_____

_____

How about the future? Do your plans follow the same path as everyone else's plans? That might look something like this:

★ Graduate high school.

★ Get into a good college.

★ Study something that interests you.

★ Meet a nice boy.

★ Get engaged halfway through college.

★ Get married soon after graduation.

- ★ Work hard at a good-paying job.
- ★ Establish a home and a career and then have 2.5 kids.
- ★ Spend twenty years shuffling kids to soccer practice.
- ★ Retire early.
- ★ Spend the last twenty years of your life enjoying winters somewhere warm and summers with your grandkids.

There's nothing wrong with that plan, exactly. But what if God showed up halfway through college and said, "Follow Me" to a mission field in Africa? What if He spoke to your heart in your first year of marriage and told you children were a blessing He wanted you to consider before you had your dream house and a bunch of money in the bank? What if He called you to a season of singleness as a young adult? What if He wanted to use your retirement years for ministry to the sick and dying? Is there room on your life map for God to ask you to follow Him in an entirely different direction?

Or are you still hoping He will follow you into the plans you have made?

I don't know what a radical faith will look like in your life. But I do know that if your future plans are all about what's in it for you, if your past looks like your present, and if you've seen Jesus on the shore and made no significant changes, you're likely still on the boat. You've traded in radical faith for shuffling dead fish.

But the ball is in your court. You can still choose radical faith. It starts with stepping off the boat.

CHAPTER 4

How to
Swim
Upstream

adical faith is faith that affects you from the top of your head to the very tips of your toes.

Radical faith changes the way you think.

Radical faith influences the way that you speak.

Radical faith moves your hands by changing what you do.

It transforms your feet by changing where you go.

Radical faith moves you out from the pew where you can simply sit and learn about God and into the world that desperately needs to see God in action.

Lindsey and Hannah know about radical faith. When Lindsey was fourteen and Hannah was fifteen, they launched a blog with a simple goal to teach other girls all that God was showing them in His Word. The blog got a lot of attention, which eventually led to a conference tour that allowed Lindsey and Hannah to teach other girls their age about what it means to have radical faith.

Lindsey says she was terrified before the first conference, but she couldn't shake the sense that what Jesus did on the cross mattered in everyday life. She wanted the chance to share that with

Radical faith moves you out from the pew where you can simply sit and learn about God and into the world that desperately needs to see God in action.

49

other girls her age. "We were both burdened by the need we saw in our generation to abandon trivial pursuits and become caught up with Jesus," Lindsey said.

Those "trivial pursuits" are the very things that keep so many girls sidelined from radical faith. Lindsey had homework to finish, friendships to maintain, and a bedroom to clean, just like every other fourteen-year-old, but she felt God nudging her to move beyond the little stuff and put first things first. She made the radical choice to make God her number-one priority and became passionate about helping other girls do the same thing.

"Of course, we did wonder, have wondered, and still wonder how God could possibly use people like us," Hannah said. "We panic way too quickly and sometimes do feel overwhelmed. Whatever happens, the results are in God's hands. We just need to be willing vessels."[4]

❀ Willing to Go

Being a "willing vessel" took Katie Davis all the way to Africa. At eighteen, she was just a girl from Tennessee when she took her first trip to Uganda. There the people and culture pried their way into her heart. She returned the next year to teach kindergarten at a Ugandan orphanage. Most would say that was radical enough, but like all radicals Katie listened to God's voice and obeyed even when He asked her to do something really big.

Katie launched a child sponsorship program, matching orphans with donors. While her peers were worrying about college finals, Katie established a nonprofit organization to meet the needs of orphans in Uganda. Two years after her first trip to Africa, Katie became a mother to three orphaned girls.

Katie went on to launch a program to feed the hungry around her. She began training women in the village how to provide for their families.

Katie is now the mother of thirteen daughters in a season of life when most young women are praying for the American dream of dream job/house/husband.

"People tell me I am brave," Katie says. "People tell me I am strong. People tell me 'Good job.' Well here is the truth of it. I am really not that brave. I am really not that strong, and I am not doing anything spectacular. I am just doing what God called me to do as a follower of Him. Feed His sheep, do unto the least of His people."[5]

"Well here is the truth of it. I am really not that brave. I am really not that strong, and I am not doing anything spectacular. I am just doing what God called me to do . . ." (katie)

Katie is referring to John 21:17. It's a passage where we find Jesus, again on the shore of a lake, talking with his first disciple: "He said to him the third time, 'Simon, son of John, do you love me?' Peter was grieved because he said to him the third time, 'Do you love me?' and he said to him, 'Lord, you know everything; you know that I love you.' Jesus said to him, 'Feed my sheep.'"

It wasn't enough for Peter to simply *say* he loved Jesus, even if he said it over and over and over. Jesus wanted Peter to know that the evidence that he loved Jesus and was a true follower of Him came from Peter's life. Specifically, Jesus said that if Peter really loved Him, he would take care of others.

This is the formula for radical faith. We listen to God's voice and read His Word, and we decide to let it impact the way that we live.

James 1:22 puts it this way: "But be doers of the word, and not hearers only, deceiving yourselves."

Radical faith makes you a doer. That means it gets you moving! It keeps you from simply reading the Bible and then walking away unchanged.

✿ Superheroes Need Not Apply

It's easy to look at these stories and feel like radical faith is impossible for us. It's tempting to believe that Jesus would never pick us to be the disciple He built His church with or call us to speak to other teenagers or adopt orphans in Africa. Surely those are missions assigned to super-Christians who memorize entire books of the Bible, never struggle with temptation, and have some sort of direct line to the heart of God, right?

 Wrong.

When we study God in His Word and listen closely to the stories of those who decide to do something big with their radical faith, a clear pattern emerges. God never calls the most-equipped person for the job. Instead, He chooses the weak in order to display His strength, and then He equips them with everything they need once they agree to get off the boat.

Lindsey and Hannah were just normal girls like you when God called them to teach His Truth to others. They admit they felt ill-equipped, but God gave them the words to say and the audience to hear them. Katie was a very unlikely candidate to become an adoptive mother. She had no children of her own, and yet God chose her to parent girls in desperate need of a mother. Remember what Peter was doing when God called him? He was just fishing. There was nothing spectacular about his life, and yet he was among the very first of the disciples Jesus called to change the world.

 The Bible is full of stories like this. Rahab was a prostitute and an unbeliever who God used to deliver His people into the Promised Land. Gideon was an insecure man from an obscure tribe, but God called him to fight an enemy army and call His people back to Him. David was a shepherd boy whose size was so unimpressive his dad didn't even consider him a candidate for king. But God had different plans. He chose David to be one of the most powerful and influential kings who would ever rule the people of Israel. Mary was a young, unmarried girl when God chose her to mother the Savior.

These people weren't superheroes. What they had in common is that they were the least likely to succeed. But they did pass the only test necessary for radical faith: They had a willingness to tell God yes.

Oh, and they also swam in the wrong direction.

✿ Swimming Upstream

I grew up near a trout farm. Hundreds of trout swam together in long pools. They all swam in the exact same direction. No trout made a ripple or dared to choose a different course from the rest of the fish.

But at the end of each pool, there were large wheels designed to pump air into the trout's water. Inside the spokes of those wheels there were grim reminders of the cost of going with the flow: dead trout that followed the current right into churning metal spikes. Eew!

So many of us Christians are like trout. We are content to swim in the same direction as everyone around us. We keep our heads down. Our ears are so plugged by the sound of the crowd that we miss the warning signs that danger is ahead or that something needs to be done.

We'd be better off to live like salmon.

Scientists have long been fascinated by a salmon's habit of swimming upstream. When it's time for a salmon to spawn (that's the fancy word for making salmon babies!), they swim upstream against currents, rocks, and obstacles in order to find the water where they were born. True, the journey is so intense that many of them die after accomplishing their mission.[6]

But they aren't needlessly ground up in a mechanical wheel they could have avoided. They choose to take the risks to accomplish their God-given mission. The trout, on the other hand, never really go anywhere. They never do much of anything. See the difference?

Everyone with radical faith has made the choice to abandon the pack, to break away from what everyone else is doing and what everyone else always has done. They've reached out and taken hold of two Truths that are clear in God's Word.

 Truth #1: The crowd cannot be trusted.

Ephesians 4:17 says, "Now this I say and testify in the Lord, that you must no longer walk as the Gentiles do, in the futility of their minds." This passage urges us not to continue to live like the crowd once we know Jesus.

The Message paraphrases it this way: "And so I insist—and God backs me up on this—that there be no going along with the crowd, the empty-headed, mindless crowd."

I hope you've got a group of great Christian friends. I want you to be plugged in to an awesome youth group where others encourage you to live like God calls you to. This passage isn't saying that the crowd can never offer wise advice or help you live out your faith. In fact, God gives us the church to help us grow in our faith. But to have radical faith, you must learn to turn down the voice of the crowd and turn up the volume on the voice of God.

Truth #2: Popularity is a trap.

Proverbs 29:25 says, "The fear of man lays a snare, but whoever trusts in the Lord is safe."

The fear of man lays a snare or a trap. What is *fear of man*? It's worrying about what other people think. It's catering to the crowd. It's doing what will make you liked and popular even when it goes against how God asks you to live.

All radicals know that trying to live for the crowd will trip them up every time.

If you want to swim upstream, you've got to reach out for God above the crowd with one hand, and grab for God above what's popular with the other hand, and trust God to move you toward His plan, even if there are obstacles to face along the way.

 It's easy to put the radicals in this book up on a platform and assume they've always been applauded for doing big things for God, but that's the romanticized version. They faced criticism, rejection, backlash, and gossip. But they swam upstream anyway, because they put first things first and made God their first priority.

In chapter 3 I told you that busyness and prayerlessness are two major roadblocks to radical faith among the young women I know. Let me add another roadblock to that list: fear of man. Remember that simply means being afraid to make an unpopular choice. It means refusing to swim upstream because you're afraid of what others might think or say.

I wonder if fear of man is standing between you and radical faith. To help you think that through, I'd like to end this chapter with some guided journaling to help you think through any areas where you may be following the crowd.

Ready? Set. Go.

✿ My Parents

If I start living with radical faith, I think my parents' reaction would be . . .

_____

_____

_____

_____

God's Truth: There are many places in Scripture where God calls you to honor your parents (Exodus 20:12, Matthew 15:4, Ephesians 6:2). It's possible your parents are not Christians or won't fully understand it if you become a "doer" of the Word. Unless your parents are asking you to make choices that are contrary to the Bible, it is your responsibility to honor them and lovingly submit to their authority. However, one of the most radical things you can do is to pray for your whole family to experience radical faith.

Let me encourage you to read the story of Paul and Silas in prison found in Acts 16:16–40. It's a great story about the power of radical faith, but in it a jailer and his entire household come to know Jesus as Lord. These verses come toward the end of that story:

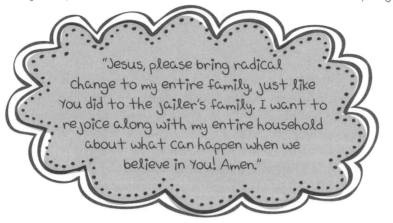

And he took them the same hour of the night and washed their wounds; and he was baptized at once, he and all his family. Then he brought them up into his house and set food before them. And he rejoiced along with his entire household that he had believed in God. (Acts 16:33-34)

If your parents are resistant to radical faith, pray:

"Jesus, please bring radical change to my entire family, just like You did to the jailer's family. I want to rejoice along with my entire household about what can happen when we believe in You! Amen."

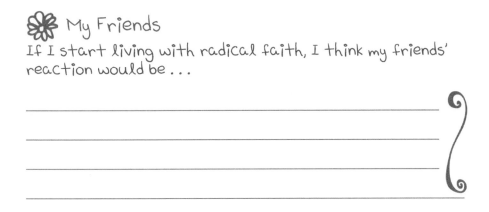

My Friends

If I start living with radical faith, I think my friends' reaction would be . . .

_____

_____

_____

_____

The Bible has a lot to say about friends. One common theme is that we need to be intentional about choosing friends who will challenge us to live more like Christ and steer clear of those friends who want to pull us toward lukewarm living.

Proverbs 27:17 suggests a great way to pray about friendship: "Iron sharpens iron, and one man sharpens another."

Wise friends will sharpen you into a better instrument to be used by God. If your friends don't encourage you to have radical faith, turn Proverbs 27:17 into your prayer: "Lord, give me friends who will sharpen me and help mold me into someone more like You. Amen."

🌸 My Peers

If I start living with radical faith, I think my peers'
reaction would be . . .

_____

_____

_____

_____

What about those people in your school who aren't necessarily your friends but you still see them every day? How about people at work or in your neighborhood who watch your life from a distance? What would they think if you started swimming upstream?

These people on the fringe remind me of one of my favorite stories in the Bible. You can read the whole thing in Luke 8:42–48. I'll give you the short version.

A woman had been sick for twelve years. She spent everything she had to try to get well, but it didn't work. Jesus was walking through a large crowd. The woman knew if she could just get to Jesus she could be healed, and so she swam upstream, literally, in order to be with Jesus.

The crowd didn't understand her. They pushed back against her. They misunderstood her. But being with Jesus was more important. He was worth the stares, the snickers, and the talking behind her back. She made it to Him and reached out to touch the hem of His cloak.

As you consider your own radical faith, I'd like you to imagine yourself as the sick woman in Luke 8. Think about the areas of your life that need Jesus' touch. Imagine all of the parts of you that you've tried to fix on your own but couldn't. Stare the crowd in the eyes. Look hard at those people who might not get it and the obstacles that stand in your way, but then shift your attention to Jesus. He hasn't chosen you because of what you have to offer. He has chosen you because of what *He* has to offer. He will give you everything you need to live like He calls you to.

keep your eyes on Him and
start swimming upstream.

CHAPTER 5

Taking
Roll

as I've been thinking about radical faith and radical followers of Jesus, I've been bowled over by a passage of Scripture I'm sure I've read a million times before: James 2:14–17.

What good is it, my brothers, if someone says he has faith but does not have works? Can that faith save him? If a brother or sister is poorly clothed and lacking in daily food, and one of you says to them, "Go in peace, be warmed and filled," without giving them the things needed for the body, what good is that? So also faith by itself, if it does not have works, is dead.

For several more verses, James goes on to wrestle with the idea that it is impossible to have faith in God and not act on it. James helps us understand the simplest definition of radical faith. Radical faith = faith in action.

Radical faith isn't just believing in God or reading your Bible now and then. It's more than simply going to church. Radical faith means your faith affects the way that you live. Without radical faith, James would say your faith is dead. Buried. In the ground. Useless.

without radical faith, James would say your faith is dead. Buried. In the ground. Useless.

As I've been thinking about encouraging you to have radical faith, I've constantly had to ask myself, "Do I have radical faith?" "Do I really live what I believe?" "Am I a doer of the Word or just a hearer?"

To be honest, I don't live radical faith perfectly. There are so many days when I prefer my iStuff to listening and responding to the voice of God. All too often, falling in line with the rest of the pack seems so much more appealing than swimming upstream. But then I remember the truths we've uncovered in this book.

★ That being a radical is required for God to use me for big things.

★ That God has called me to have hot faith, not the maintenance-free kind that tastes like lukewarm water.

★ That this world is not my home, and that only what is done for Christ will last.

★ That Jesus was a radical too.

And suddenly I want to step in line with Elijah, Joshua, Peter, and Paul. I want to scream, "Pick me!" for a radical mission for God's glory. I hope this has become your heart's cry too.

I know what you're thinking: What next?

If I'm the coach and you're my team, I've just given you the game-changing pep talk. I hope you're fired up and ready for a faith that changes how you live. But I'm sure you want to know what the plays are. You want to know exactly what radical faith should look like in your life.

Here's the bad news: I can't tell you what comes next. Because radical faith is the result of listening to God and obeying, there is no such thing as cookie-cutter radical faith. While there are some things that are true for all Christians, radical faith may look different for each of us.

Remember my farm? We moved there directly from a house in the city. When we loaded up the U-haul, we left behind a busy life chock-full of commitments, responsibilities, meetings, and busyness. We made the radical choice to move after reading this passage:

And in fact, you do love all of God's family throughout Macedonia. Yet we urge you, brothers and sisters, to do so more and more. Make it your ambition to lead a quiet life, to mind your own business and to work with your hands, just as we told you, so that your daily life may win the respect of outsiders and so that you will not be dependent on anybody. (1 Thessalonians 4:10–12 NIV)

We immediately saw several ways we could become doers.

★ We could seek to love God's family more and more.

★ We could make it our ambition to lead a quiet life.

★ We could work with our hands.

★ We could intentionally build a life that would win the respect of those who don't know Jesus.

We saw pulling back from the pace of normal life as just one way we could make God our first priority. And so we bought a farm and some goats and some chickens and now live a life that is radically different from the one we'd imagined.

But not everyone is called to goat farming.

Some Christians are called into the very heart of a city to minister to the people there. Some are called to reach out to their neighbors in the area where they already live. Some are called to pick up the pace in ministering to others. Some are asked to slow down so they can hear the voice of God.

Do you see what I mean? We can't churn out radical faith on an assembly line. I can't tell you exactly what radical faith will look like for you. But if radical faith is faith in action, anyone can be a radical.

The truth is, God is really the coach in this scenario. He's the one calling the plays. I'm on the team just like you are. But I can give you a peek at the playbook. Here come five "mini chapters" that will help you turn up the heat on your faith as soon as you close this book.

Let me encourage you to read them slowly. Don't speed through them. It's not a race. Take your time. Listen for God to speak. Ask Him to show you His radical plan for your life.

❀ #1 Hear God

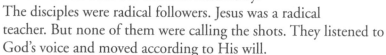

What's the number-one thing you can do to move away from lukewarm faith? Listen to God.

Think back to all the radicals we've examined in this book. Elijah was a radical prophet. Joshua was a radical warrior. Paul was a radical missionary. The disciples were radical followers. Jesus was a radical teacher. But none of them were calling the shots. They listened to God's voice and moved according to His will.

Do you want to be a radical Christian? You must listen to God.

What? does God sound like? How can you know if you're hearing from Him?

We often wait for some mystical message from God. We expect Him to download His mission into our brains in the same way we get songs on iTunes. God can speak to us that way if He wants to. There are examples in the Bible of God speaking directly to someone or revealing Himself through an angelic visitor or vivid dream, but the most common and consistent way to hear from God is by reading His Word.

As I look back, the habit that has made the biggest difference in my life has been reading the Bible. I'm a little bit all over the map on how I do it. Sometimes I read in the morning, sometimes late at night. Sometimes I track what I'm learning in a journal. Sometimes I don't. Sometimes I follow a Bible-reading plan or use a Bible study; sometimes I just open and read. But when I read I expect to hear from God, and I look for ways to apply what I've read (that's being a doer versus a hearer!).

The Bible is a big book and it's not always easy reading, so I understand if the thought of reading the Bible more overwhelms you. To get you started, here are five simple reading plans that can help you hear from God by reading His Word.

> The most common and consistent way to hear from God is by reading His Word.

Read the Bible in a Year

Choose a Bible specifically designed to help you study the Bible over the course of the year or Google "365 day Bible reading plan" for a guide for how to read the entire Bible in one year.

Bible Biographies

If you love to read biographies, try studying the people in the Bible. You can learn a lot about who God is by studying how He interacts with and responds to people. Here are a few of my favorites:

♥ Eve: Genesis 1–3

♥ Jonah: Book of Jonah

♥ Ruth: Book of Ruth

♥ Hannah: 1 Samuel 1–2

♥ John the Baptist: Matthew 3, 11, 14, 17; Mark 6; Luke 7; John 1, 3

♥ Nicodemus: John 3:1–21, 7:50–52, 19:38–42

Read Two Books at a Time

Read one chapter from an Old Testament book and one chapter from a New Testament book every day. Keep reading in order until both books are finished, and then pick two more books to study.

Story Time

Jesus was a great storyteller. He often preached about deep truths in parables or stories. Make a commitment to read all of Jesus' parables found in the New Testament. You can Google "Jesus' parables" for a complete list.

Read the Gospels

Matthew, Mark, Luke, and John record Jesus' time on earth. These four books are often called "the Gospels." It's a good habit to read through the Gospels regularly. These are the books that record Jesus' life, ministry, and death. If you've been a Christian long, it can be easy to be desensitized to Jesus' story. Read these books often. You'll be amazed every time at how Jesus lived.

ACTION STEP: I will read the Bible more by . . .

_____

_____

_____

 #2 Obey

What separates radicals from everyone else is that they obey when God speaks. Elijah confronted the prophets of Baal when God told him to. Joshua blew the trumpets when God gave him the green light. Paul obeyed God's order to stop persecuting Christians.

If you're going to have radical faith, you need to obey God when He speaks.

Are there areas of your life where you sense God is asking you to make a change, but you are resistant? If so, do not pass Go. Do not collect $200. Do not rush through this chapter without stopping to obey.

A radical obeys God no matter what the cost is. If you're ready to be radical, it's time to say, "Yes, Lord."

♡ ACTION STEP: I will obey God by ...

_____

_____

_____

❀ #3 Make Room

Remember that sweet girl from the Gallery who cried at the altar because of her math homework? My guess is that many of you can relate more to her than to the radicals you've read about in this book.

You're busy. You're stressed out. You're tired. Your schedule is jam-packed. You're anxious. You're so busy treading water, you've got no energy to swim upstream. For you to get radical, you're going to have to turn down the noise. Something's gotta give.

What can you bow out of to make more room for God in your life? What can you step back from in order to step up to the plate of radical faith?

This step may be painful. You may need to give up something you love. You may wrestle with your feelings about yourself if your identity is tied to achievement and accomplishment.

But you can't be a radical and stay in the pack. Take it from a recovering busyness addict: Once you give yourself some breathing room, you'll be in for the God-sized adventure of your life.

ACTION STEP: I will turn down the noise in my life by taking a break from . . .

_____

_____

✿ #4 Plug Your Ears to the Crowd

There may be some voices you need to stop listening to. There may be some friendships that need to be put on the back burner, some bands you need to unplug from, some shows you need to stop watching in order to find the courage to follow God's plan.

There may be some shows you need to stop watching.

Take some time to evaluate who or what encourages you to have faith in action and who doesn't. Remember that the crowd cannot always be trusted. They may very well push you in the wrong direction. Ask God to show you that He matters most and to help you worry less about what others think. And while you're at it, ask Him to give you friends who are radical followers of Jesus.

ACTION STEP: I will value the opinions of God above the opinions of . . .

_____

_____

_____

❀ #5 Be a Follower

Remember those first disciples? They were minding their own business when Jesus showed up and called them to something radically different. You may feel like you've had a similar experience as you've read this book. Suddenly it's clear that you can't coast, that following Jesus will cost you, that He wants more from you than business as usual.

Jesus is asking you to be His follower. Remember that's not the same as asking Him to follow you as you go about business as usual.

I wish we could talk to those disciples. I'd love to pick their brains about that moment on the shore, but I'm fairly confident I can speak for them on the matter of radical faith. I'm sure they'd tell us it was worth it. They'd urge us to ditch our own dead fish and follow Jesus, wherever He leads.

If you want radical faith, it's time to tell Jesus you don't need to be in the lead. Tell Him you want to follow Him wherever He goes. Tell Him you're ready to give up your dead fish.

♡ ACTION STEP:
I will live my life like Jesus is in charge.

🌼 Roll Call of Radicals

Earlier in this book, I took roll. I started rattling off the names of radicals found in the Bible. Of course, it wasn't a complete list. I could never name all the people who have done radical things with their faith. But if I could, I'd like to add your name to the list. I'd lump you with the Elijahs, the Joshuas, the Pauls, the Peters, the Lindseys, the Hannahs, and the Katies. I'd proudly tell the tales of the ways you've put your faith in action and made a difference by following hard after God.

It's my dream to see young women everywhere rising up to radical faith—to see you ditching the idea that lukewarm faith has anything to offer and getting fired up about putting your faith in action.

I can't imagine what could change if each of you asked God to radically use you, but I'd sure like to find out. Will you ask God to change you into a radical? Will you put first things first and do what it takes to seek God's kingdom first?

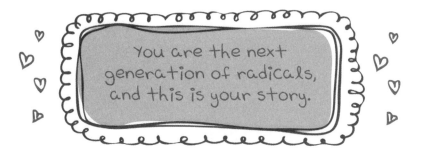

"Yes, Lord!"

I can hear your collective, "Yes, Lord," and it makes my heart want to burst.

You are the next generation of radicals, and this is your story.

NOTES

1. Merriam-Webster, "radical," www.merriam-webster.com/dictionary/radical.

2. Bob Arnot, "Dr. Bob: Perfect Water Temp for Hydration," *Men's Journal*, March 23, 2010. http://archive.mensjournal.com.

3. Marcia Clemmitt, "Students Under Stress," *CQ Researcher*, July 13, 2007, 581. www.cqresearcher.com.

4. Debra Weiss, "Real Interview: Beauty from the Heart," RealTeenFaith.com, May 19, 2009. http://realteenfaith.com.

5. Katie Davis, "Katie's Story," Amazima.org, accessed December 26, 2012. www.amazima.org.

6. Robert Jones, "Why Do Salmon Swim Upstream?" *How It Works*, July 13, 2011. www.howitworksdaily.com.

Acknowledgments

My momma taught me better than to receive a gift without sending a thank-you note. This series is the end result of many gifts—people who love me well, friends who cheer me on, and fellow Jesus-lovers who consistently point me toward God's Truth. If you fit into one (or all) of those three camps, this page is my thank-you note to you. (Be sure to mention to my mom that I sent it!)

The Gab Gallery. I loved the girls I met during the research phase of this book. Your openness and honesty helped me know what to write. You also encouraged and inspired me by proving my suspicions that God is using young women to do big things. Keep letting Him use you. I'm on the edge of my seat waiting to see what mountains God will move with your generation. I did not get to meet all of you personally; instead some of you had the treat of hanging out with my friend, Dree. Speaking of . . .

Dree. Dree was my focus-group leader for the book. She hung out with girls in places like Little Rock, Springfield, and Tulsa. Anyone who had the chance to spend time with Dree knows what a treasure she is. Dree, I credit you with giving me the Truth bug. Your passion for God and His Word is positively infectious. Thanks for consistently pressing me to choose God's Truth and to live my life according to His Word. If we were back in junior high, I'd want you to wear the other half of my BFF necklace.

Holly, René, and Team Moody. I am so thankful for a publishing team who believes in the message of God's Truth and entrusts me to deliver that message to young women. Your kindness bowls me over. Thank you.

Jason, Eli, and Noble. At the end of the day, I am Jason's wife and Eli's and Noble's mom. These are the roles that bring me the most joy and force me to keep running to God's Word for answers. My sweet family listened to endless readings as this work evolved from an idea into a four-book series. When the process got stressful, they did things like make me a leaf pile and invite me to jump in. Family, I adore you. You are the very best part of my story.

Jesus. Thank You, Jesus, for being so completely irresistible.

Also available as ebooks

MOODY
PUBLISHERS

978-0-8024-0644-6   978-0-8024-0642-2   www.MoodyPublishers.com   978-0-8024-0643-9   978-0-8024-0643-9

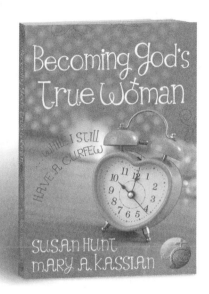

Becoming God's True Woman

Who did God make you to be? What kind of person will you become? What does God's word say about things like beauty, friendships, guys, and dating?

Also available as an ebook

MOODY
PUBLISHERS

978-0-8024-0360-5

www.MoodyPublishers.com